To my sister Leigh, who gave me an early
introduction to appendicitis.

And special thanks to the Wolofsky family,
good friends and appendicitis experts.
Thanks for all your help.
—L.B.F.

For my family for all of their love and support
while I was in the hospital. For my mom for
all of her sleepless nights. For my husband,
Josh, for fighting to be heard. For Elliot whose
mommy was "far away in the hospital."
And for Juliette, my sweet baby girl.
—J.K.

by Laurie Friedman
illustrations by Jennifer Kalis

 Carolrhoda Books   Minneapolis • New York

CONTENTS

A WORD FROM MALLORY

I, Mallory McDonald, officially love starting a new year. But this year, I officially love it even more than ever.

NOT because Mom is having her special New Year's Eve dessert party, which includes chocolate pie with mini marshmallows on top. (My favorite!) NOT because Max and I get to stay up until midnight and celebrate. NOT because Dad is buying blowers and shakers and hats for everyone (even my cat, Cheeseburger). NOT because Grandma is here for a visit. And NOT even because it might snow, and when it does, my street, Wish Pond Road, will look like a winter wonderland (Mom's words, not mine).

This year, I, Mallory McDonald, am officially more excited than ever about starting a new year because this year my friends from summer camp are coming to stay at my house for a winter reunion.

Carine, my bunkmate from last summer at Camp Blue Lake, and Taylor, Mary Ann's bunkmate, are coming to Fern Falls and staying at my house for three days and two nights. Mary Ann is sleeping over too, and we're going to plan all kinds of things to do. Mary Ann says it is going to be fun, fun, fun, and I say my best friend is right.

We haven't seen our camp friends since last summer, and we can't wait for them to get here. And the good news is that we don't have to wait much longer. They're coming the day after tomorrow!

FOUR girls. THREE days. TWO nights. If you ask me, there's not ONE thing that could get in the way of a great time.

TEA FOR TWO

"Mallory, would you like some tea?" asks Grandma.

Mom and Grandma look cozy at the table with the teapot and the basket of muffins that Grandma baked, but right now, I have other things on my mind besides tea. "Sorry, I don't have time for a tea party," I tell Grandma.

Grandma puts a muffin on a plate and pushes it toward me. "I think this blueberry muffin has your name on it."

Grandma winks at me.

No matter what kind of muffins Grandma makes, she calls them Mallory muffins. She knows I like that.

I pick a blueberry out of my Mallory muffin and pop it into my mouth. "Grandma, my camp friends will be here in two days, and I have to start getting ready for our reunion. Anyway, haven't you ever heard the expression . . . *tea for two*?"

Mom and Grandma both laugh. Then Grandma takes a sip of her tea. "I have heard that expression, but I think a tea party can be as big or as small as you want it to be."

I smile at Grandma. "I wish I had time to make this *tea for three*, but I really do have a reunion to plan."

"At least finish your muffin," says Grandma.

I take a tiny bite out of my muffin, and then I put it down on my plate. "Grandma, you know how much I love Mallory muffins, but today, I just don't have any room." I pat my tummy to show her that it's full. When I do, it kind of hurts.

"Mallory must still be full from the waffles you made for breakfast," Mom says.

Grandma smiles. "When I come to visit, I guess I do get a little overly excited in the kitchen. Visits are just so much fun."

I get up and give Grandma a big hug.

"I love when you come to visit us," I tell her. And there's another visit I'm going to love . . . Carine and Taylor's. But I don't know how much they're going to love it if I don't get busy planning.

There's someone who needs to help me plan, and that someone is Mary Ann.

I start to pick up the phone, but my brother, Max, grabs it before I do. "Important business," he says like whatever he's got to do on the phone is more important than what I've got to do. Max walks into the laundry room with the receiver and slams the door behind him.

I know Max is going to call our next-door neighbor Winnie. I don't think that's more important than planning a reunion, but once he gets on the phone with her, I know it will be forever before he gets off, so I sit down at the desk and start typing.

Subject: M.E.!
From: malgal
To: chatterbox

Mary Ann,

Hey! Hey! Hey! Help! Help! Help! I'm having an M.E. (short for *Mallory Emergency*, in case you forgot). Carine and Taylor are going to be here in 2 days, and we still don't know what we're going to do. Just thinking about it makes my stomach hurt! Actually, it might be hurting from all the waffles I ate for breakfast. I don't know, but it's definitely hurting. OK. Enough about my stomach. Are you going to help me?

Puh-leeeeze G.O.H.A.S.A.P.A.H.M.S.P. (short for *Get over here as soon as possible and help me start planning*)!

Mallory

I push the *send*
button and look at my
watch. I wonder how
long it will take for my
email to get to Mary
Ann. It shouldn't take

too long. It only has to go next door.

While I'm waiting for Mary Ann to write
back, Grandma asks me about my camp
friends. "Mallory, I'd love to hear about
the girls who are coming to visit."

I grin. "I'd love to tell you about them,"
I say to Grandma.

I start telling her all about my summer
at Camp Blue Lake. "Mary Ann and I met
Taylor, one of the girls who is coming to
visit, on the bus on the way to camp. She
ended up being Mary Ann's bunkmate.
Then I met my bunkmate, Carine. I didn't
actually like her at first, but then we got

to be B.B.B. Now, all four of us are really good friends."

Grandma looks a little confused. "It all sounds good," she says. "The only thing I'm not sure about is the B.B.B. part."

I laugh. "Sorry, Grandma. That's short for *best, best bunkmates.*"

Grandma nods like she gets it now. "It sounds like there's nothing that can get in the way of the four of you having a wonderful time together."

"Grandma, you're right. We are going to have a great time together."

Grandma laughs. "Well, you know what they say . . . *Grandma knows best.*" She gives me another little hug.

When I hear my computer say *You've Got Mail,* I race back over to the desk. Return mail from Mary Ann. Yeah! I click on her email and start reading.

Subject: Winter Reunion
From: chatterbox
To: malgal

What does a girl have to do to use the phone around here!?! Winnie has been on it all morning (with your brother)! Do you think she actually likes talking to him? I mean, you're his sister and you don't even like talking to him. I don't get it!?!

OK. On to important things. I can't wait for our reunion to start! We're going to have so, so, so much fun! And yes! Yes! Yes! I will help you plan everything. That's what best friends are for.

I.W.B.T.A.S.A.I.F.C.M.R. (short for *I will be there as soon as I finish cleaning my room*)! C U Soon!

Mary Ann

I smile as I read her email. Mary Ann and I have been best friends since the day we were born. We used to live next door to each other until I moved to Fern Falls. I still can't believe her mom married Joey and Winnie's dad, and now we're next-door neighbors again.

"Someone sure looks happy," says Grandma.

"I am," I tell Grandma. "I'm happy my best friend lives next door to me, and I'm happy my camp friends are coming to visit."

Just thinking about how much fun I had at camp last summer with all my friends makes me super happy.

"Tell me something," says Grandma. "Who came up with the idea of having a winter reunion?"

Max walks back into the kitchen, puts

the phone down on the desk, grabs a muffin out of the basket, and takes a big bite. When he does, crumbs fall all over the floor.

"Whoever made these muffins should be rewarded," says Max. He smiles and gives Grandma a big hug.

Then he looks at me and frowns. "Whoever came up with the idea of having a reunion should be punished," he says. "I can't believe I have to spend the next three days with a house full of girls."

"I thought you like girls," I say to Max.

Max takes another bite of his muffin. He rolls his eyes and gives me an *I-like-some-girls-but-your-friends-definitely-aren't-on-the-list* look.

"The reunion was my idea," I tell Grandma proudly.

Max grunts like he's never heard a worse idea.

I ignore Max and his grunting. My brother might not be too excited about my winter reunion, but I can hardly wait for the fun to begin!

PLANNING TIME

Knock. Knock. Knock.

Someone is knocking on my window, and I know who that someone is. There's only one person who knocks on my window, and that person is Mary Ann.

"Password please," I mouth through the glass.

Mary Ann puts her mouth right up to the window. "Open up, it's freezing out here!" she shouts loudly enough for me to hear her through the window.

That isn't the password, but I open my window anyway. When I do, two things rush into my room . . . a blast of cold air and Mary Ann.

She has a notebook and a pen. "I'm ready to start planning our winter reunion," she says with a smile.

I get out my paper, clipboard, and pens, and we sit down on the floor of my room.

"OK. We've got three days of planning to do, and every day needs to be fun, fun, fun," says Mary Ann.

"That's one fun for every day," I say.

We both laugh at my joke. Then we get busy planning.

We work for a long time on our schedule. We make lists of what we're going to do and what we're going to eat. We even write down what we're going to wear and where we're going to sleep.

WINTER REUNION
FLOOR PLAN

BAD IDEA PILE

The good ideas stay on my clipboard, and the bad ones end up in a scrap pile on my floor.

While we're still busy deciding which TV shows to watch and what movies to rent, Mom sticks her head into my room. "Who's ready for a hot-chocolate break?" she asks. She brings two steaming mugs of hot chocolate into my room and sets them down on my desk.

"Yum!" says Mary Ann. She jumps up and helps herself to one.

"None for me," I say.

Mom frowns. "Since when have you said *no* to hot chocolate?"

"I'm just not in the mood today," I tell Mom.

Mom looks at me like she's concerned. "Sweet Potato, you said *no* to muffins, and now, you're saying *no* to hot chocolate. Do you feel OK?"

Mary Ann pats me on the back with her hot chocolate-free hand. "She feels fine," she says with a big grin. "She's just so busy planning our reunion that she doesn't have time to stop for hot chocolate."

Even though I'm not so sure my stomach does feel fine, maybe Mary Ann is right.

"We still have to email Taylor and Carine," I tell Mom.

"And make the *Welcome* sign," Mary Ann reminds me.

Mom nods her head like she's satisfied with our answers. "I'll let you girls get back to work." Then she smiles at me. "I'll leave the hot chocolate here in case you change your mind."

"Thanks, Mom," I say.

After she leaves, Mary Ann and I get back to work.

I give Mary Ann a box of markers. "Why don't we start on the sign, and when we're done, we'll email Taylor and Carine."

"Great plan!" Mary Ann spreads a long piece of sign paper out on my floor.

I outline the letters, and Mary Ann starts coloring them in. "This is fun," she says as she colors.

I finish outlining and help her color. Getting ready for our reunion is fun, but I know it won't be as much fun as the real thing.

When we're done coloring, we spread out our sign along my bed.

WELCoME TO FERN FALLS, Carine & Taylor!

"I love our sign," says Mary Ann.

"Me too!" I say.

We both stand back to admire it, but while we're busy admiring, we hear a knock. This time it's on my bedroom door. And the someone knocking doesn't even wait for me to say come in.

Max walks into my room with his dog,

Champ. Champ curls up under my desk with Cheeseburger, and Max plops down on the bed right on top of our sign.

"Hey!" I say while I try to grab the sign from underneath him. "Can't you see you're sitting on a sign?"

Max shrugs like he doesn't care what he's sitting on. "I've got a weather report."

"Don't you mean a *love* report?" Mary Ann laughs. She likes teasing Max about Winnie.

Max does what he usually does when Mary Ann says anything: he ignores her. He tosses a baseball up into the air with one hand and catches it in the other. "It's supposed to start snowing tomorrow."

"Did someone say snow?" My next-door neighbor, Joey, walks into my room.

Mary Ann starts jumping up and down and throwing all of our little pieces of scrap paper up in the air. It looks like it's already snowing on Joey.

"It's going to be so much fun!" screams Mary Ann.

Max holds his hands over his ears. "I don't know how much fun anything can be with the two of you screaming like that."

Actually, it's just Mary Ann screaming, but when she screams she's so loud, it sounds like we're both screaming.

Mary Ann keeps jumping up and down and screaming. "If you think that's loud, just wait till Carine and Taylor get here," she says to Max.

Max rolls his eyes. "Don't remind me that they're coming."

"Don't worry," says Mary Ann. She holds up our official planning notepad. "We've got lots of plans, and none of them include you."

"Do they include a trip to the zoo? Because that's where the four of you belong."

I try pushing Max off the bed, but when I do, I feel a pain in my stomach. "We're all staying right here having fun together," I tell my brother.

Max rolls his eyes and then rolls off my bed. "C'mon, Joey. I think the boys better stick together for the next few days."

Joey picks scrap paper out of his hair and follows Max into his room. Mary Ann and I go into the kitchen. "Time to email," I say.

Mary Ann pulls a chair up to the desk. I rub my stomach and start typing.

Subject: Winter Reunion!
From: malgal, chatterbox
To: carineluvsgreen, taylortalks

Hi Carine and Taylor!

It's Mallory and Mary Ann, and we're writing to say we can hardly wait for you two to get here and for our winter reunion to begin. We've got everything planned out (down to the last piece of popcorn). We don't want to tell you too much because we want it all to be a big surprise, but here are a few things we do want you to know:

Thing #1: We're all sleeping at my (that's me, Mallory's) house. There are so many of us, it'll be just like sleeping in a cabin but without the counselors. (There's a mom and dad up the stairs, but that doesn't really count.)

Thing #2: Bring your hats and mittens. It's supposed to snow in Fern Falls, and we're going to be very busy outside playing in it.

Thing #3: Wear your Camp Blue Lake T-shirts. We'll look just like we did at camp (except instead of wearing shorts and flip-flops with it, we'll have on coats and boots).

OK. That's it for now. We don't know how we're going to be able to wait for the day after tomorrow to get here. WE CAN'T WAIT 2 C U!

Mallory and Mary Ann

When we're done writing, I click the *send* button. "Even though we've never planned a winter reunion before, I think we're pretty good at it."

Mary Ann nods her head like she agrees.

"We could probably write a book," I say. *"How to Plan a Winter Reunion with Your Camp Friends."*

"If we did, our book would have a happy ending," says Mary Ann. "This is going to be the best, best, best reunion ever."

I high-five Mary Ann. I couldn't agree more. With all the plans we made, there's nothing that can get in the way of our having a great time.

THE COUNTDOWN

The minute I wake up, I look at my clock and start counting down.

8:30 a.m. *(25 hours and 30 minutes to go before official winter reunion begins!)*

I pop out of bed and pull my curtains aside. No signs of snow yet. I close my eyes and pretend that I'm at the wish pond on my street.

I wish the snowflakes will get here before my friends do.

Carine and Taylor are arriving at 10:00 a.m. tomorrow, and I can hardly wait. Everything's going to be perfect once they get here, and it will be even better than perfect if there's snow on the ground.

I hug Cheeseburger, brush my teeth, put on a sweatshirt and leggings, and rub my stomach, which still hurts.

8:42 a.m. *(25 hours and 18 minutes to go before official winter reunion begins!)*

When I walk into the kitchen, I do ten things.

Mallory's List of 10 things she does When she walks into the kitchen:

Thing #1: Kiss Mom, Dad, and Grandma.

Thing #2: Skip Max.

Thing #3: Take banana out of bowl.

Thing #4: Put banana back in bowl. (Stomach not in the mood for bananas.)

Thing #5: Feed Cheeseburger.

Thing #6: Try not to throw up while feeding Cheeseburger.

Thing #7: Stick finger in bowl of whatever Mom is baking and lick finger. (Stomach not even in the mood for cake batter either.)

Thing #8: Think about telling Mom Stomach hurts.

Thing #9: Decide not to. (Don't want Mom to cancel reunion due to tummy ache.)

Thing #10: Check to see if I have email.

And the good news is . . . I do! I have
an email from Carine and one from Taylor
too. I click on my inbox and start reading.

Subject: Packed and ready to go!
From: carineluvsgreen
To: malgal, chatterbox

Hi Mallory and Mary Ann!
I can't believe I'm coming to Fern Falls . . .
TOMORROW! I'm already packed and ready
to go. I have my hat, mittens, Camp Blue
Lake T-shirt, and the answer is YES, lots of
other stuff too. My mom said it looks like I'm
going away for 3 months, not 3 days! But
who cares, I can't wait to go!
I'm sooooo excited!!!
Carine
P.S. Mallory, I can't wait to see your room.
I can't wait for tomorrow to get here!

When I'm done reading the email from Carine, I click on the one from Taylor.

Subject: One more day!
From: taylortalks
To: malgal, chatterbox, carineluvsgreen

Hi girls!

Just one more day till reunion time! It's going to be SUPER FUN, FUN, FUN! I wanted to bring Tickles, but Dad said cats stay home, and girls go to reunions. Oh well.

I can't wait 2 C U!

Love,

Taylor

P.S. Mallory, I can't wait to meet Cheeseburger! Meow!

10:19 a.m. (*23 hours and 41 minutes to go until official winter reunion begins!*)

TRANSCRIPT OF WHAT'S HAPPENING IN
THE MCDONALD KITCHEN:

MOM: Mallory, can you please
get the butter and eggs out of
the refrigerator. I'm baking a
chocolate pie, a strawberry cake,
apple tarts, and lemon cookies for
our New Year's Eve party.

MALLORY: (what she's thinking but
not saying as she gets the butter
and eggs out of the refrigerator)
Even though I love all those things,
none of them sound good right now.

MAX: Mom, how are we supposed to
wait till New Year's Eve to eat all
that stuff?

MOM: (smiling and chopping apples) I can't wait till the last minute to do all the baking.

DAD: (talking to Max) You'll be too busy doing other things, like making New Year's resolutions, to have time to eat all the baked goods.

MAX: (rolling his eyes) Dad, don't start this year with the whole *you've-got-to-find-ways-you-want-to-change-yourself-for-the-better* routine.

DAD: Making resolutions at the start of the New Year is important.

MALLORY: (phone rings) I'll get it. (listens then says) Hold on

a minute. Hey Max, it's Joey. He
and Mary Ann want to know if we
want to go next door and play
some games.

MAX: Count me out.

MALLORY: Winnie is playing too.

MAX: (shrugging shoulders like
he doesn't really care if goes even
though everyone in the room knows he
can't wait) I guess I'll go.

MALLORY AND MAX LEAVE TO GO NEXT
DOOR TO THE WINSTON HOUSE. (MAX
LEADS THE WAY.)

11:05 a.m. *(22 hours and 55 minutes until official winter reunion begins!)*

"Monopoly or Twister?" Joey says when he opens the door.

"Monopoly," Mary Ann and I say at the same time.

Max ignores Mary Ann and me. "Let's play Twister," he says, looking at Winnie.

Winnie opens the box and starts setting up the Twister mat. I start to say that I know why Max and Winnie want to play Twister, but Max gives me a *keep-your-mouth-closed* look before I even have a chance to open it.

Joey spins and we all take turns twisting. I have my right hand on blue and my left hand on red, but when I try to put my right foot on green, I feel like someone is playing a game of Twister in

my tummy. "I think I'm going to sit this one out," I tell everyone.

When they finish playing Twister, we cram onto the Winstons' couch to watch TV.

"This is boring," Winnie says after a few minutes.

"Yeah," says Max.

"Does he agree with everything she says?" Mary Ann whispers loudly enough to me for Max to hear.

Max looks like he's about to shove Mary Ann off the couch, but before he does, Joey's dad walks into the family room with a big bowl of popcorn. "Since you're all bored, maybe it's time for school to start again," he says.

"NO!" we all scream at the same time.

3:34 p.m. *(18 hours and 26 minutes until official winter reunion begins!)*

My stomach officially hurts.

What I do: lay down on the couch in my living room and watch TV with Cheeseburger. What I don't do: say anything to Mom. I know she'll want to take me to the doctor or say something mom-ish, like "Maybe your friends shouldn't come to visit if you have a stomachache."

6:15 p.m. *(15 hours and 45 minutes until official winter reunion begins!)*

Dinner at the McDonald house. I just pick at mine.

"Mallory, eat your chicken," says Mom. "You've hardly had anything all day."

"I made it especially for you," says Grandma.

I push chicken and peas around on my plate. Even though I really don't feel great, I really don't want Mom and Grandma to think something is wrong.

"I think I'm just too excited about the reunion to be able to eat," I say.

Dad laughs. "Well, I hope you're not too excited about the reunion to be able to make some New Year's resolutions."

Max groans. "It's not even New Year's yet. Why don't we eat dessert now and make resolutions later?"

Mom laughs. Then she puts a plate of lemon cookies on the table. "I knew it was a mistake to bake early."

Max shoves a whole cookie into his mouth. "It was definitely not a mistake," he tells Mom.

We all laugh. But when we do, my stomach does that Twister thing again.

9:30 p.m. (*12 hours and 30 minutes until official winter reunion begins!*)

"Good night, Sweet Potato." Mom kisses my cheek. "When you wake up, your friends will be on their way."

Dad rumples my hair. "And Wish Pond Road should be a blanket of white."

I try to smile at the thought of our street covered in snow. I try to think about the sleds and shovels that Max set up in the garage, and the hats, sunglasses, carrots, and buttons to make snowmen with that I put in a box by the front door. But I have a pain in my stomach that's making it hard for my mouth to smile.

"Mallory, is everything OK?" asks Mom.

I nod. I really don't want Mom to cancel this reunion because my tummy hurts. "I just have a little stomachache, but I don't think it's anything," I say.

Mom looks concerned, but Dad smiles. "I'm sure those are butterflies flying around in your tummy, and they'll land just about the same time your friends do."

"I think you're right," I tell Dad.

I hug my parents good night and turn out the light. I do hope that tomorrow Wish Pond Road will be a blanket of white, but what I really hope is that tomorrow, my stomach will feel much better than it did today.

AN APPLE A DAY

Good news: Wish Pond Road is a blanket of white.

More good news: My friends will be here in a few minutes.

Bad news: My stomach doesn't feel any better today than it did yesterday.

More bad news: It feels a whole lot worse.

I think about an expression that Mrs. Daily, my teacher from last year, taught us. *An apple a day keeps the doctor away.*

I take an apple out of the fruit bowl in the kitchen and take a bite. But it doesn't help.

"Mallory, how are you feeling this morning?" Mom asks.

Before I have a chance to answer, I hear a horn honking outside. I grab my coat, leave my uneaten apple on the counter, and run out the front door. Carine and Taylor are already getting out of Carine's dad's van.

"MALLORY!" They both scream at the same time.

"CARINE! TAYLOR!" I run toward my friends.

"You're here! You're here! You're here!" yells Mary Ann. She runs across her snowy yard to my driveway, and we all start jumping up and down and hugging.

Well, some of us jump. If my stomach could talk, it would say, *"I'm not in the mood to jump."* So I don't.

Even though one part of me, the stomach part, doesn't feel so good, the rest of me is super excited to see my friends that I haven't seen since last summer. "I thought our reunion would never get here," I say.

Carine loops her arm through mine. "Take me straight to your room! I can't wait to see where the world's best bunkmate, otherwise known as Mallory McDonald, lives."

Taylor giggles. Then she sticks one arm through my empty arm and her other one through Mary Ann's. "And we can't forget about her famous cat."

"WE'RE GOING TO HAVE SO MUCH FUN!" yells Mary Ann as we start to walk into my house.

I look up and down Wish Pond Road to see if any people come running out of their houses when Mary Ann screams. She's loud enough for everyone on our street to hear her. I can tell Carine's dad thinks she's loud too.

"You have an amazing outdoor voice," he says to Mary Ann.

We all laugh and walk inside.

Mom invites Carine's dad to come inside for coffee.

"Welcome to Fern Falls!" Grandma says to everyone.

Carine's dad has a cup of coffee. Then he says he wants to get back on the road in case it snows some more. He gives Carine a big hug. "I'll see you in three days, Sweetheart. And Happy New Year!"

When Carine's dad leaves, I rub the place on my stomach that hurts. It doesn't actually help very much, so I try to focus on something besides my stomach. "I can't believe we get to celebrate New Year's Eve together!" I say to my friends.

"Wait till you see everything Mallory's mom baked," says Mary Ann.

"I can't wait to see it," says Taylor.

"I can't wait to taste it," says Carine.

I try to laugh, but it hurts when I do. "You don't have to wait much longer," I tell my friends. "Our New Year's Eve party is tonight."

"I can hardly wait!" says Carine. She picks up her suitcase and hands me her pillow and teddy bear. "C'mon, I also can't wait to see your room."

When we get there, Carine picks up everything on my desk and looks at it.

"Who wants a reunion schedule?" I ask.

"First, I want to see everything in your room," says Carine.

"And I want to see your cat," says Taylor. She scoops Cheeseburger up off of my bed. "Aw, she's even cuter than the picture you showed me last summer."

"OK. Now let's talk about everything that's happened since camp," says Carine when she's done inspecting all the photos and jewelry on my dresser.

We all plop down on my bed. Actually, Carine, Taylor, and Mary Ann all plop. I try to, but my stomach won't let me plop. I sit down slowly.

Mary Ann tells Carine and Taylor how she moved to Fern Falls over the summer and started school with me this year. "It's so cool that Mallory and I are next-door neighbors just like we used to be before she moved to Fern Falls."

Carine tells us that she's taking an art class. "I'm really into it," she says. "And my mom lets me hang all of my paintings in the living room."

Taylor tells us she plays the saxophone in a band.

"Mallory, what about you?" asks Carine.

I tell my friends about the class trip to Washington, D.C., that Mary Ann and I went on. Then I shrug my shoulders. "Besides this reunion and that trip, nothing exciting has happened to me in a long time."

Carine smiles. "Maybe something will soon."

"Maybe something exciting will happen during our reunion," I say.

Taylor and Carine cheer like they like that idea. Mary Ann looks at her watch. "OK, enough with the cheerleading. Mallory, you pass around the schedules."

I give everyone a copy of the schedule that Mary Ann and I made. "First activity, snowman building," I tell my friends. I fold my schedule into a little square and stick it into my back pocket.

"Last one to put on her hats, boots, and mittens is a rotten egg!" says Taylor.

We all get dressed quickly and then take the box of snowman accessories I put together and go outside.

"OK, to make the perfect snowman, we need a big ball, a medium ball, and a little ball," says Mary Ann. She takes over like she's in charge of building the snowman.

Which is fine with me. Even though I'm happy that my friends are here and we're all together playing in the snow, I'm having a hard time thinking about building the perfect snowman. My stomach is starting to really hurt.

"Let's work on the big ball first," says Mary Ann.

We all start rolling snow into a big ball. When we're done with the big ball for the bottom, we start rolling a medium-sized ball for the middle.

"Hey! I have an idea," says Mary Ann. "Why don't we make a snow family."

"I love that idea," says Carine. "We can make a dad and a mom and a brother and a sister snowman."

"And a cat." Taylor smiles at me like she knows I'll like that idea.

But right now, the only idea I like is to go inside and lie down. My stomach feels terrible.

I stop rolling snow and watch while Mary Ann, Taylor, and Carine keep going. When they're done with the ball for the middle, they start rolling a smaller snowball for the head.

"Our snowman needs a face," says Taylor. She takes a carrot and two buttons out of the box I brought outside and sticks them on the snowman. "Now he's got eyes and a nose," she says.

"He needs clothes too." Carine pulls a hat out of the box and sticks it on his head.

"The only thing he's missing is a name. C'mon girls, let's think." Mary Ann makes an *I'm-trying-to-think-of-the-perfect-name* face.

I make a face too. But I guess it's not an *I'm-trying-to-think-of-the-perfect-name* face, because all of a sudden, my friends look at me like thinking of a name is the last thing on any of their minds.

"Mallory, you don't look so good," says Taylor.

"Are you OK?" asks Carine.

"Maybe we should go inside," says Mary Ann.

I bend over and clutch my stomach while my friends help me walk inside. Even though a tummy ache is the last thing I want to have, I officially have one.

When we get inside, I lie down on the floor of my kitchen and hold my stomach. I try not to cry, but I can already feel the tears starting to roll down my face.

"You look sick!" says Mary Ann. She uses her outdoor voice to call Mom, and it works. Mom is in the kitchen in no time.

In even less time, she's on the phone with my doctor. Then, she starts asking me questions. "Mallory, which side does it hurt on? Mallory, does it hurt more when you touch it or when you let it go? Mallory, can you hop around like a bunny?"

I answer Mom's questions. The pain is on the right side. It hurts more when I let it go than when I touch it. I'm not hopping anywhere.

Mom tells the doctor my answers. Then after lots of *uh-uhs* and *I sees*, she hangs up. Mom has a serious look on her face.

"I'm fine, right?" I wait for Mom to say that I am, but something about the look on her face doesn't make me feel so fine.

"Mallory, we need to go to the emergency room," she says. "Dr. Bruce thinks you might have appendicitis."

Now I really start to cry. I'm not even sure what appendicitis is, but it doesn't sound like something I want to have.

"I can't go to the hospital," I tell Mom. "My friends just got here."

"Mallory, I'm sorry," says Mom. She reaches down and helps me up off the floor.

"But we're making a snow family and we just started." I look at Mom and try to give her my best *please-don't-make-me-go-to-the-hospital-and-have-appendicitis-while-all-my-friends-are-here-making-a-snow-family* look.

But it doesn't work. Mom doesn't look any happier about going to the hospital than I do.

She puts an arm around me. "Mallory, I'm sorry, but we need to go to the hospital. And we need to go now."

As I wave *bye* to my friends and let Mom help me into the car, I think about the conversation I had this morning with my friends in my room.

When I said what I did about something exciting happening to me at our reunion, this was not at all what I had in mind.

A CHANGE
OF PLANS

I pull a piece of paper out of my back pocket and hand it to Mom. "Spending the morning in the emergency room is NOT on the schedule that Mary Ann and I made!" I say between tears. "I want to be at home with Grandma and my friends, not at the hospital."

Dad rubs my back. "Sweet Potato, getting sick and going to the hospital is never on anyone's schedule."

I moan and clutch my stomach. I usually feel better when Dad calls me Sweet Potato, but today just hearing the word makes me feel like I'm going to throw up. "I don't think I'll ever want to eat again," I say.

Mom kisses my forehead. "You'll feel better soon."

I shake my head like I can't believe what she's saying could be true.

"Your mom is right," says a nurse.

She's the same nurse who took my *vitals* and did my *blood work* and then took me to *radiology* for a *sonogram.* I had never heard these words before this morning, and now I sound like I went to medical school.

"The doctor will be here in just a minute," the nurse says.

"The doctor is already here. I'm Dr. Hart," says a kind-sounding voice from behind me. He walks into the room and shakes

Mom's and Dad's hands. "You must be Mallory," he says to me.

I nod my head just a little. Even though I usually like being me, today I'd like to be anybody but me.

"Mallory, I have some pictures I'd like to show you and your parents."

Dr. Hart flips a switch, and a white box on the wall lights up. "This is called a light box," says Dr. Hart. "And it will help us see the pictures we took of you earlier."

"No one took pictures of me this morning," I tell Dr. Hart. I am definitely not in the mood to have my picture taken today, and I would remember if someone tried.

Dr. Hart smiles. "Actually, these are X-ray pictures and we took them of your appendix." He puts some black-and-white pictures up on the light box.

"If you ask me, whoever took these pictures didn't do a very good job. I can't even tell what they are," I say.

Dr. Hart smiles at me. "It's a good thing I'm here because it's my job to explain the pictures to you." He points to something on the X-ray that looks like a blob. "This is your appendix," says Dr. Hart. "A healthy appendix is about the size of a walnut."

I look at the X-ray. "It's kind of hard to tell what it is, but it looks a lot bigger than a walnut," I say.

Dr. Hart has a concerned look on his face. "Unfortunately, your appendix looks more like a grapefruit than a walnut."

I clutch my stomach again. "I don't know why everyone keeps talking about food."

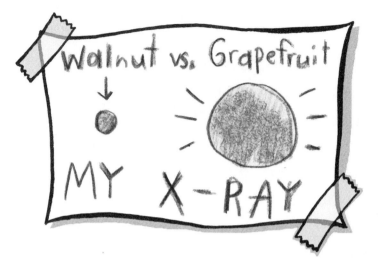

Walnut vs. Grapefruit

MY X-RAY

Dr. Hart looks like he's sorry that I'm uncomfortable. "I'm sure food does not sound appealing right now. I know your stomach hurts."

He pauses, like he does not want to say what comes next. "I'm sorry, Mallory, but we need to remove your appendix immediately."

Then he looks at Mom and Dad. "We're going to give her something for the pain now, and we'll perform the surgery as soon as an operating room opens up."

Dad nods like that makes sense to him, but it doesn't make any sense to me.

I wipe away my tears. "You can't just take out my appendix!" I say to Dr. Hart. "Isn't it like an arm or a leg or a head? Don't I need my appendix?"

Dr. Hart smiles like he's trying to make me feel better. "Mallory, the good news is that you do not need your appendix to live a healthy life. In fact, you will feel even healthier without it."

I can feel the tears starting again. "Well, you can't take out my appendix today." I wipe my eyes with my sleeve. I don't want to keep crying, but it seems like all the tears in Fern Falls are in one place . . . falling down my face.

I tell Dr. Hart about all the plans Mary Ann and I made. I tell him how much I've missed my camp friends and how long I've been waiting for our reunion to get here. "Can't we wait and take out my appendix next week after my friends leave?"

Dr. Hart looks sympathetic. "If we wait, your appendix will rupture, and we don't want that to happen."

"I don't even know what *rupture* means, but it can't be that bad."

"Unfortunately, it is," says Dr. Hart. "Rupture is a medical term, which means to explode. We don't want your appendix to explode while it's inside of you. Mallory, I know this is not what you want to hear, but your appendix needs to come out today."

I give Dad a *please-tell-this-doctor-we're-going-to-wait-until-next-week-to-take-out-my appendix* look.

Dad hugs me like he understands that this is upsetting to me. "Mallory, I'm sorry, but we need to do what Dr. Hart says."

I shake my head from side to side. "I don't want to get my appendix out today. Actually, I don't think I want to get my appendix out at all. It sounds scary."

Dr. Hart pats my hand. "You don't have to worry about anything. I'm going to perform the operation. I take out hundreds of appendixes every year. The surgery won't take long, and before you know it, you'll be as good as new."

Even though I don't want to have my appendix out, hearing that I will be as good as new is the best news I've heard all day.

I look at my watch. "Will I be good as new by 3 p.m.?" I ask Dr. Hart. "That's when my friends and I are making friendship anklets and drinking hot chocolate with extra marshmallows."

"I'm sorry Mallory, it's going to take a little longer than that," says Dr. Hart.

A little longer than that. I look at Mom. "How long is it going to take? I need to go home. I want to be at my reunion."

Mom puts her arm around me. "Mallory, I know you want to be with your friends, but right now, we need to focus on your appendix."

The nurse comes back into the room and hands Mom and Dad a clipboard and a pen. They start reading and signing papers.

I look down at the schedule in my hand. Mary Ann and I made so many fun plans.

I lay back on the examining table. A tear falls from my cheek onto the white paper cover.

I spent so much time imagining what the reunion would be like.

I imagined Mary Ann, Taylor, Carine, and me playing outside in the snow, having snowball fights, and building snowmen.

I imagined us curled up around the fireplace, drinking hot chocolate, and eating popcorn.

I imagined us eating desserts and celebrating New Year's Eve together.

I imagined the four of us in my bedroom, all snuggly and warm in our pj's, laughing and telling stories.

But of all the things I imagined, I never, ever, ever imagined I'd be in the hospital getting my appendix out. If you ask me, that is unimaginable.

OPERATION A

When I open my eyes, Mom and Dad are standing over me. Dad bends down and kisses my forehead.

"Where am I?" I mumble.

Mom tucks my hair behind my ears. "You're at Fern Falls Children's Hospital," she says softly. "You just had your appendix out."

I reach down to feel my tummy. On the outside, it hurts a little when I press on it, but the inside feels better. "I think the pain is gone," I tell my parents. My voice comes out much more quietly than it usually does.

Dad squeezes my hand. "Operation Appendix complete, and you did great."

I swallow. My throat feels dry. "Can I have something to drink?"

Mom smiles and hands me a little cup of ice chips. "Take things slowly," she says. "You're still weak from the operation."

I put an ice chip in my mouth, and when I do, everything that happened starts popping up like flash cards in my brain. My stomach hurting. My street filling up with snow. Mom baking for the New Year's Eve party. My friends coming to town for a winter reunion. All of us building a snowman. Me going to the hospital. I start to sit up in the bed, but Dad stops me.

"I need to go home to be with my friends," I say.

"Relax, Sweet Potato. You need to rest and recover in the hospital," says Dad.

The hospital is not where I want to be. I want to be at home.

"I'll rest for a little while," I tell Dad. "But I need to get back this afternoon. My friends and I are making friendship anklets, and we're going to decorate the house for the party. Isn't tonight New Year's Eve?"

Mom and Dad look at each other. Then Dad picks up my hand. "Mallory, tonight is New Year's Eve, but you just had an operation. You're going to need to spend the night in the hospital. If all is well, you should be able to go home tomorrow afternoon."

I can feel the tears starting to form in the corners of my eyes again. "*Tomorrow afternoon!* I can't wait that long. If I have to stay here, I'll miss New Year's Eve and

the party tonight and I won't get to be part of the reunion that I helped plan."

Dad squeezes my hand. "Mallory, I know this is hard for you, and it's not what you planned, but sometimes things . . ."

I know Dad is about to say *happen*, but I don't give him a chance to finish. I want him to understand that I need to be at home, not here. "What about Cheeseburger? I need to take care of her."

"We talked to Grandma. She's taking very good care of everyone at home, and she said Taylor is helping her take care of Cheeseburger," says Dad.

"I want to see Cheeseburger, and I want to be with my friends!" I tell Dad. I try to sit up in bed like I'm planning to get out of it and go home. But I don't get very far.

Dad helps me settle back down against the pillow. "Mallory, a cat can't come to the hospital, but if you're feeling up to it later this afternoon, we can try to arrange for your friends to come visit," Dad says.

"I want to be with my friends at home. Having them visit me in the hospital was not part of our reunion plans," I tell my parents.

Mom takes a deep breath, like she's trying to be patient, but I'm not making it easy. "We know," says Mom. "But seeing your friends a little bit is better than not seeing them at all."

I start to tell my parents how disappointed I am, but my mouth feels too sleepy to say anything else. I close my eyes.

When I open them, someone is standing over me. She's wearing a white nurse top and hat. For a minute, I think I'm outside playing in the snow and this is a snow lady, but then I realize I'm not outside and this is no snow lady.

"Hello Mallory, I'm Nurse Nancy, and I'll be taking care of you while you're recovering at Fern Falls Children's Hospital."

Nurse Nancy smiles and then sticks a thermometer in my mouth. "Dr. Hart says you were a real trooper and did great during the operation." She takes the thermometer out of my mouth and adjusts some tubes that are sticking into my hand. Then she shows me a little button I can push if I need to call her for anything.

"Everything looks fine," says Nurse Nancy. She pats my arm. "The doctor will be by in a little while to check on you. But you can call me if you need anything."

Mom and Dad thank her, and I push the call button before Nurse Nancy even has a chance to leave the room.

Nurse Nancy turns around and smiles. "Most kids like to push that button," she says. "What can I do for you, Mallory?"

I tell Nurse Nancy about my reunion and how I was supposed to be at home with my friends having fun, not in a hospital recovering from an operation. "I was just wondering if my friends can come visit me in the hospital this afternoon?"

Nurse Nancy looks like she feels sorry for me. "Mallory, I wish I could say *yes*, but you're going to have to wait and ask Dr. Hart."

I cross my toes under the sheets. "I really want my friends to come visit,"

I say to Mom and Dad after Nurse Nancy leaves.

Mom gives me a *we-understand-how-you-feel* look. "We'll ask the doctor when he gets here."

Dr. Hart walks into the room. "Does someone have a question for me?"

"I do." I raise my hand that isn't connected to tubes. I remind Dr. Hart about what I was supposed to be doing today. Then I ask my question. "I want to know if my friends can come visit later."

Dr. Hart smiles. "Let's check you out first. Then I'll give you an answer. Now, let's take a look at that tummy."

Actually, I kind of want to look too. I haven't seen what my tummy looks like now that it doesn't have an appendix in it.

Dr. Hart moves my hospital gown to the side.

"Except for some bandages, my tummy looks pretty much the same as it did when it had an appendix in it," I say.

Dr. Hart laughs as he inspects my stomach. "Removing an appendix is not such a big deal." He removes my bandages and points to three small cuts on my stomach. "All you have are three incisions," he explains. "One in your belly button, one beneath your belly button, and one on your right side above your hip."

"Everything looks just as it should," says Dr. Hart. He takes three fresh Band-Aids out of his coat pocket and places them carefully on my incisions.

I look down at my tummy. The Band-Aids he puts on are pink, and they have little hearts on them. "Those are so cute," I say to Dr. Hart.

He grins. "They're my special '*hart*' Band-Aids. Why do you think everyone calls me Dr. Hart."

I'm confused. "Isn't Dr. Hart your real name?"

Dr. Hart laughs. "It is, but when I saw the heart Band-Aids, I couldn't resist."

"It's a good thing your name isn't Dr. Pickle. Pickle Band-Aids might have been hard to find."

Dr. Hart laughs again. "I'm glad to see we only removed your appendix, and not your sense of humor," says Dr. Hart. He pats me on the shoulder. "I'll come back to check on you a little later."

He starts to leave the room, but I stop him before he has a chance to go.

"Dr. Hart, you forgot to answer my question. Since everything looks just as it should, do you think my friends can come visit me in the hospital this afternoon?"

Dr. Hart scratches his head like he's considering my request. "Mallory, I think that is a fine idea," says Dr. Hart. "But they can't stay too long. You need your rest."

I nod my head like that won't be a problem.

Mom smiles. "Your friends can come a little later. But now, you need to get some rest."

I yawn. "I am kind of sleepy," I tell Mom. I put my head back on the pillow and smile. Even though this isn't how I planned my reunion, I can't wait to see my friends.

A LEMON
OF A VISIT

"Jell-O and clear fluids time!" says Nurse
Nancy.

She walks into my room and puts a tray
down in front of me. When she does, the
red Jell-O in the bowl starts wiggling like
it's in a Hula-hoop contest. I look at the
clear fluid. It looks like chicken soup with
way too much water in it.

I take a little bite of Jell-O. "When is

it going to be *friends-come-visit-me-in-the-hospital* time?" I ask.

Nurse Nancy looks at her watch. "Visiting hours begin in a little while."

I put down my spoon. "I can't wait to see my friends."

Nurse Nancy smiles. "And I'm sure they can't wait to see you. They came all the way to Fern Falls to be with you, and I bet they're just as disappointed as you are that you're not at home with them."

Wow! I've been so busy thinking about how I feel, I haven't even thought about how my friends are feeling. I bet Nurse Nancy is right. I bet my friends are so sad I'm not at home with them. I can just imagine what they've been saying.

Nurse Nancy interrupts my thoughts. "You won't have to wait much longer for your friends to arrive. I think I hear them in the hallway."

"MAL-LOR-Y!" Mary Ann, Carine, and Taylor all say together. They're the first ones in my room, but Max, Joey, Grandma, and even Winnie aren't far behind.

"Honey Bee!" says Grandma when she sees me. She bends down and gently

wraps her arms around me. "I don't want
to hug you too tightly," she says.

"You won't hurt me," I say with a smile.
I'm so happy to see everyone, I can't
imagine anything hurting, especially a hug
from Grandma.

Carine, Mary Ann, and Taylor all give me
a group hug.

"I can't believe you had to have your
appendix out," says Joey.

"Did it hurt?" asks Max.

"I'm sorry you're stuck in the hospital
over winter break," says Winnie. She
makes a face like she really is sorry. "So
what was it like to have your appendix
taken out?" she asks.

Everyone is being so nice, even Winnie.
I start telling them about the operation
or, at least, what I remember about the
operation, which isn't much. "It seems

like I got to the emergency room this morning and the next thing I knew, I woke up in a hospital room and my appendix was out."

"That doesn't sound too bad," says Carine.

"You look a lot better than you did this morning," says Taylor.

"We were all really worried about you," says Mary Ann. Then she holds up a big shopping bag. "We have loads of goodies for you!"

Taylor, Carine, and Mary Ann all crowd around my bed. They give me cards that they made and a big stack of fashion magazines and game books.

"We wanted you to have something to do while you're here," says Taylor.

Mary Ann pulls some hair thingies and lip gloss out of the bag. She puts a clip in my hair and opens a tube of lip gloss for me to put some on.

This visit is making me even happier than I thought it would.

"Your grandma told us you have to sleep here tonight," says Carine.

"I wish I didn't," I say. "I'd rather be home celebrating New Year's Eve with all of you."

Taylor, Carine, and Mary Ann put their arms around each other and crowd around me. "Well, we all wish the same thing," says Carine.

"Yeah," says Taylor. "We're all going to stay up late tonight, and we're going to have so much fun, but it would be a whole lot more fun if you were there too."

Wait! Stop! All of a sudden, this visit went from *happy* to *NOT*.

Hearing Taylor say, *"We're going to have so much fun"* was not at all what I expected her to say. I know she was trying to make me feel better, but just hearing that they're going to be staying up late and having fun without me makes me feel worse.

"Hey, let's show Mallory what we made this afternoon," Carine says to Mary Ann and Taylor.

They all giggle and count to three. Then they all put their feet in the air. "We made matching friendship anklets," says Taylor.

"And we made one for you too," says Carine. She pulls a friendship anklet out of her pocket and hands it to me.

"Thanks," I say. I look down at the anklet in my hand. Even though I think

it's sweet that my friends made it for me,
I would have rather had no anklet and
heard them say, *"We were too sad to do*
anything without you, especially something
as much fun as making friendship
anklets."

"Aren't they cute, cute, cute?" says
Mary Ann. "When we get home from the
hospital, we're going to watch old episodes
of *Fashion Fran.* Then we're going to start
decorating the house for the party."

"That sounds great!" I try to smile like
I'm glad they're having fun without me, but
the truth is, I'm not really all that glad.

I think about what Nurse Nancy said
about my friends being sad that I'm not
at home with them. I'm sure she knows a
lot about cuts and Band-Aids, but I don't
think she knows anything about friends
and winter reunions. It doesn't seem like

my friends are sad at all that I'm here and they're there.

Mary Ann looks at Carine and Taylor. "I can't wait to decorate for the party. Everything is going to look great, great, great!" she says.

Max rolls his eyes. I know he can't stand listening to Mary Ann say anything even once. He really hates it when she says things three times. And for the first time, I understand how he feels. Each time Mary Ann says "*great*," I feel *worse*.

Max interrupts my thoughts. "Joey and Winnie and I brought you something too." He hands me a bag.

I open it and pull out a little stuffed cat. "Thanks!" I say.

"We got it downstairs in the gift store," says Winnie.

"We thought you'd like it," says Joey. "It looks like a mini Cheeseburger."

Just hearing the name *Cheeseburger* reminds me of my cat. "How's Cheeseburger doing?" I hope my cat is OK with me gone.

"Cheeseburger is adorable!" says Taylor. "She hasn't left my side all day." Taylor smiles. "Every time I pick her up, she purrs. I think she likes me."

Carine giggles again. "Taylor even made a friendship anklet for Cheeseburger."

I try my hardest not to frown. I know my friends think I'll feel better knowing that my cat is being taken care of, but I don't feel better at all. I feel worse than I did before. Not only are my friends having fun without me, but my cat is too!

"Hey Mallory, since your new cat looks like a mini version of Cheeseburger, why don't you name him Slider, like the mini hamburgers," says Joey.

"I think that's a perfect name," says Dad. "Mallory, what do you think?"

"Sure," I say, like I think that's a great idea. But right now, I can't think about naming a stuffed cat when all my brain can think about is my real cat and my real friends who are having a great time without me.

Dr. Hart walks into the room. "I'm sorry to be the bearer of bad news," he says. "But it's time to end the visit. The patient needs her rest." Dr. Hart stands by the door and holds it open like he's waiting for everyone to leave.

Everyone says good-bye. Mary Ann, Taylor, and Carine all hug me. "We're sad, sad, sad to go," they all say together.

But as soon as they get out in the hall, I can hear them all laughing and talking. I even hear them ask Grandma if they can have hot chocolate when they get home. If you ask me, they don't seem sad at all.

"That was a nice visit, wasn't it?" asks Mom.

Dad rumples my hair. "I'm sure our little patient was very happy to see her friends." Dad looks at me, like he's waiting for me to say that I'm happy, but I don't.

Mom slides my tray of food toward me. "Why don't you try to drink a little more. You need some fluids," she says. "You can pretend that you're at a tea party."

I take a little sip, put down the cup, and frown.

Mom and Dad look at each other.

"Mallory, I know you want to be with your friends on New Year's Eve and that you're upset that things didn't work out the way you wanted them to," says Dad.

I look up at the ceiling. It looks like a sea of white tiles. I start counting them. *One. Two. Three. Four.* "That's not the only reason I'm upset."

Dad pushes my hair behind my ears. "Sweet Potato, you want to tell me what's bothering you?"

I go back to counting. *Five. Six. Seven. Eight.* "It just seemed like my friends weren't even that sad that I'm not with them. They were all laughing and having fun when they left," I say softly.

"Honey, they told you that they're sad you can't be with them tonight. And I'm sure they are. I know it's disappointing that they're together and you're here, but if all goes well, you'll be home with your friends tomorrow," says Mom.

Nine. Ten. Eleven. Twelve. I think about my friends who are home celebrating New Year's Eve, eating desserts, and watching the ball drop while I'm stuck in the hospital counting ceiling tiles. "It was going to be so much fun staying up until midnight and ringing in a new year with my friends, and now, they're doing it without me."

Dad sits down on the edge of my bed. "Sometimes things happen that you don't expect, and when they do, you just have to make the best of it."

I go back to counting. *Thirteen. Fourteen. Fifteen.* "I don't see how you make the best out of being stuck in a hospital and missing the reunion you planned with your friends who you haven't seen for months and won't see again until next summer."

Mom sighs, like she's trying to find a good way to explain it to me. "Have you ever heard the expression, *When life hands you lemons, make lemonade?* It means you should try to make the best of a bad situation."

I don't answer. I look across my room at the stretch of ceiling tiles.

I've heard that expression, but if you ask me, my visit with my friends was a whole lot more lemons than it was lemonade.

TEA FOR ONE

What's a girl to do if she's stuck in the hospital on New Year's Eve while all her friends are at her house having fun and eating dessert without her?

A. Eat Jell-O and drink clear fluid.
B. Try to escape.
C. Reread the magazines her friends bought her.
D. Write a sad story.

I've already done A, B, and C, so I ask
Mom for a piece of paper and start on D.

TEA FOR ONE,
by Mallory Louise McDonald

[NOTE #1 TO READER: Only read this if
you like stories with sad endings.]

Once upon a time, there was a poor,
sweet, darling girl who had planned a
winter reunion with all of her friends.
She worked long and hard to make sure
everything would be just right. All she
wanted was to have fun holidays and
ring in the New Year with her friends.
But that's not what this poor, sweet,
darling girl got. Instead, she got an
operation.

[NOTE #2 TO READER: You've only read the first paragraph, and don't you think it's a sad story already? Well, it gets worse.]

The girl's parents and a mean doctor told her she had to have her appendix out. They didn't ask her if she wanted to have her appendix out. They didn't ask her if it would be convenient for her to have her appendix out. They didn't even say, "*May we please take your appendix out?*"

Good at operating.
Bad at listening!

Nope. All they said was, "We have to operate today."

When the girl said today was not a good day for her to have an operation because she already had plans with her friends (she even showed them the paper with her plans on it), plus it was New Year's Eve (which seemed like a terrible time to have an operation), all they said then was, "Wait here and we'll let you know when there's an available operating room."

[NOTE #3 TO READER: Stop here and go get some tissues.]

I bet you think that things couldn't get much worse for this poor, sweet, darling girl, but they did.

After she had her operation, her friends came to visit her, which she thought would cheer her up, but it only made her feel worse because it made her wish she was at home with them and not stuck in a hospital by herself. Plus, it didn't seem to her that her friends were even one bit sad that she wasn't with them.

[NOTE #4 TO READER: Here's the sad ending I warned you about.]

Then the girl's mother told her to do all sorts of beverage-related things, like make lemonade and have a tea party.

The girl didn't feel like doing either of those things. (Who would if they had just had their appendix out?) But being the sweet, darling girl that she was, she did as she was told. (OK. She didn't actually make the lemonade, but she did have a tea party.)

She had a tea party for one and sipped her clear fluid, even though doing so reminded her of her friends at home who were having their own tea party (or in this case, a hot chocolate party).

THE END.

Hot Chocolate vs. mug-o-nothing
U pick!

[NOTE #5 TO READER: Aren't you glad I made you go get the tissues?]

Portrait of a poor, sad girl all alone on New Year's Eve

AN IMPATIENT PATIENT

Brrrring.

At first, I think that sound is my alarm going off in the morning, but when I open my eyes and look around, I realize I'm not in my room at home and that sound is not my alarm clock. It's the telephone in my hospital room.

I look out the window, and it's bright and sunny. The last time I looked out the window, it was dark and cloudy.

Mom shakes my shoulder. "Mallory, phone call for you," she says.

"I don't even remember falling asleep last night," I say to Mom.

She smiles. "Operations have a way of making you very sleepy," she says.

I take the receiver from Mom and say hello.

Mallory: Hello.

Grandma: Good morning, Honey Bee. How are you feeling today?

Mallory: I think a little bit better.

Grandma: That's wonderful. I have some girls who would like to speak to you.

Mary Ann: Hey! Hey! Hey! That's one hey from me, one from Carine, and one from Taylor.

Mallory: Hey! Hey! Hey! That's one hey back for each of you.

Mary Ann: We want to know if you're coming home today.

Mallory: I don't know yet, but I hope so.

Mary Ann: Don't hang up. Carine and Taylor and I have a surprise for you.

Carine, Taylor, and Mary Ann (all singing into the phone to the tune of "Happy Birthday"): Happy New Year to you! Happy New Year to you! Happy New Year, dear Mallory! Happy New Year to you!

Mallory: Thanks! Happy New Year to you too! How was the party last night?

Mary Ann: Um, well, I um . . . I better not tell you too much about it. We'll tell you about it when you get home. But we have to go now. We're busy, busy, busy! Hurry home! Bye! Bye! Bye! That's one bye from each of us.

I say *bye* and hang up the phone.

Something about that phone call bothered me. Actually *several* somethings about that phone call bothered me.

First of all, Mary Ann wouldn't even tell me about the party last night. They probably had such a good time, she didn't want to talk about all of the fun I missed.

And second of all, my friends were so busy doing things, she didn't even have time to stay on the phone and talk to me. She might as well have said, "Mallory, the reunion is lots of fun with *or* without you."

That phone call made me feel like if I don't get home soon, they won't remember that I'm part of this reunion. I throw back the covers and start to get out of bed, but Mom stops me. "Where are you going, young lady?"

"I'm going home." I remind Mom that Dr. Hart said I could go home today.

Mom smiles. "You can't just leave the hospital. You have to be discharged."

"I don't even know what *discharged* means, but I know I'm ready to get home."

Mom laughs. While she explains that being discharged means being released by the doctor to go home, Nurse Nancy walks into my room.

"Happy New Year, Mallory!" she says. "How is the patient feeling this morning?"

"Ready to go home!" I say. I stretch my arms up over my head to show that I feel well enough to move around.

Nurse Nancy sticks a thermometer in my mouth. "I know you're anxious to get home to your friends. Dr. Hart will be by shortly. You know the drill. You have to ask him."

Since I can't talk with a thermometer in my mouth, I nod my head that I understand. As soon as Nurse Nancy takes the thermometer out of my mouth, I ask her if she will see if Dr. Hart can come check on me now.

"Dr. Hart is here!" he says cheerfully. "Happy New Year!" he says to Mom and me. "How is the patient feeling this morning?" he asks.

I stretch my arms and wiggle my toes. Then I reach down and touch my tummy where my appendix used to be. "All fine. Can I go home now?"

"I need a little more information than that," says Dr. Hart.

"All of me feels good, even though my stomach is still a little sore right here." I point to the area where the incisions are.

"That's normal," says Dr. Hart.

"Great! Now can I go home?" I start to sit up in bed, but Dr. Hart stops me.

"Not so fast, young lady. I need to examine you, and then we can make that decision."

Dr. Hart pulls back the covers and peels the little heart bandages off of my tummy. "Your incisions are healing nicely," he says.

"Double great!" I say. "Now can I go home?"

Dr. Hart starts putting new bandages on my incisions. "I can see that our patient is not very patient this morning. I know you want to get home to see your friends." He finishes changing my bandages, then pulls the covers back up. "I'd like you to eat some breakfast this morning and walk around a little bit. If you can do that without a problem, then you can go home. Sound like a fair deal?"

I nod my head that it does. "I just have one question," I say to Dr. Hart.

"Yes, Mallory, what is it?" he asks.

"Is it time for breakfast yet?"

Dr. Hart and Mom both laugh like I was trying to be funny.

They might think I was joking around, but I wasn't. As far as I'm concerned, I only have two things left to do at this hospital.

One. Eat breakfast.

Two. Leave.

A SURPRISE CELEBRATION

I don't know which feels better:

A. Walking out of a classroom at the end of a school year.
B. Finishing your liver and onions when your mom says, "Clean your plate."
C. Going home from the hospital after you've had an operation.

Even though all those things feel really good, I think I'll have to go with C. I'm still not my normal self, but I feel a lot better than I did yesterday. All I want to do is to get home to see what I've been missing out on.

"We sure will miss you around here," says Nurse Nancy. She gives me a little

teddy bear and a card that says *I* ♡ *Fern Falls Children's Hospital.* She gives Mom a bunch of papers to sign and some medicine for me to take later.

"Thanks for taking such good care of me," I say to Nurse Nancy.

Nurse Nancy gives me a hug good-bye. "I know you're excited to go home and see your friends." Then she winks at me. "There's a nice gift shop in the lobby. I know how much your friends mean to you, and I'm sure you mean a lot to them. Maybe you want to take a look and see if you can find a little something for them before you leave."

"What a wonderful idea," says Mom.

When we get to the lobby, Mom takes me to the gift shop.

I try to stop her. "C'mon," I say tugging on her arm. "All I want to do is go home."

But Mom doesn't look like she's in a hurry to leave. "These are awfully cute," she says.

I know that the fastest way to leave is to agree. "Those are really cute," I say. I pick up what Mom is pointing to, and we pay. The only thing I want to do in this gift store is leave it. I just want to go home.

But as soon as we get into the van, I start to feel a little differently.

"Mom, I think it's weird that nobody would tell me about the party last night," I say. "Do you think everyone is scared to tell me about it because I missed something that was so much fun?"

Mom looks like she's more focused on driving home safely from the hospital than she is on answering my question.

Even though I couldn't wait to get home, now I'm not so sure that's where I want to be. It doesn't seem like my friends missed me while I was gone. I reach down and rub the fur on Slider's back. Maybe I should have stayed at the hospital.

I pull my reunion schedule out of my pocket. "When I get home, my friends and I are going to play outside in the snow and then drink hot chocolate," I tell Mom.

Mom looks like she doesn't like that idea. "Mallory, you're still weak. All you need to be doing for the next few days is resting."

I frown. "My friends are going to be playing in the snow and drinking hot chocolate and having fun. How can I be part of the reunion if all I'm doing is resting?"

Mom turns on to our street. "Don't worry, Sweet Potato. I'm sure your friends will think that just being with you is fun."

But I am worried. What if my friends want to do things that I can't do? I take a deep breath. This reunion isn't turning out at all like I planned.

As we pass the wish pond on my street, I close my eyes tightly and make a wish. *I wish the rest of my reunion will be lots of fun, just like I planned.* I keep my eyes shut for a minute. I really want this wish to come true.

When I open my eyes, Mom is pulling into the driveway.

She honks the horn. Dad, Grandma, my friends, all of the Winstons, and even Max come running outside.

"We missed you so much!" says Carine.

"Cheeseburger, say *hello* to Mallory!" Taylor holds my cat up and wiggles her paw back and forth so it looks like she's waving to me.

"Wish Pond Road was too quiet without you," says Joey.

"Honey Bee, we're all so glad you're better," says Grandma.

Colleen and Frank and Joey's grandpa all give me hugs.

Mary Ann loops her arm through mine. "C'mon!" she says. "We have something for you."

I see what the something is as soon as I walk inside.

The welcome sign that Mary Ann and I made for Carine and Taylor is gone. There's a new sign hanging in our living room that says, "HAPPY NEW YEAR, MALLORY!"

"Surprise!" everyone says at the same time.

"Sorry we couldn't spend more time talking to you this morning, but we were busy getting ready for your homecoming," says Mary Ann.

I look at the sign. "Wow! I love it!" I say. "What a great surprise!"

Grandma puts her arm around my shoulders. "That's not all," she says. "Your friends have lots of surprises for you."

Mary Ann plops a pointy New Year's hat with fringe on it on my head.

"HAPPY NEW YEAR, MALLORY!" they shout together and blow on blowers.

Everyone puts on their hats. The hats have little signs sticking out of the top that say, *Happy New Year, Mallory.* Joey even puts a little hat on his dog Murphy's head, and Max puts one on Champ and Cheeseburger.

I laugh when I see them, and Mom takes a picture.

"Come look in the dining room," says Grandma.

When I do, I'm confused. All the desserts

that Mom made for New Year's Eve are there, and no one has taken a bite. "How come no one ate any of the desserts that Mom made?" I ask. "Wasn't the New Year's Eve party a *dessert* party?"

Dad smiles and puts his arm around me. "No one wanted to celebrate New Year's Eve without you. And even though the party is a dessert party, it just wouldn't have been sweet without you. So we waited. This year, we're celebrating on New Year's Day, instead of New Year's Eve."

I think I'm getting unconfused. "You waited for me to have the party?" I say with a smile. I look at Mom, and she nods her head like that's exactly what they did.

Carine and Taylor and Mary Ann all nod too.

"It wouldn't be any fun without you," says Carine.

"We've been busy all morning getting everything ready," says Taylor.

"We even recorded the ball dropping in Times Square," says Joey. "So it's kind of like we're celebrating New Year's Eve on New Year's Day."

"It's going to be so, so, so much fun! We can all watch together," says Mary Ann.

All of my friends start screaming and jumping up and down.

Now I understand why nobody would tell me about the party. There was nothing to tell. They hadn't had it yet. And I know why Mary Ann couldn't stay on the phone and talk. Everyone was too busy getting ready for me to come home.

Just thinking about everyone thinking about me makes me feel really good. One by one, I give everyone a hug.

"I'm glad you're home, Honey Bee," Grandma says when I hug her.

"I'm glad I'm home too," I tell Grandma. "It's a good place to start a new year."

Max puts his fingers in his mouth and whistles. "Enough hugging. Let's eat!" he says. "I don't know how I've waited this long."

Max takes a lemon cookie from the table and pops it into his mouth. When he's done with his cookie, he gives a plate to Winnie so she can get some dessert.

Mary Ann rolls her eyes. "All of a sudden, Max is Mr. Polite-and-Romantic," she whispers to me.

Mary Ann is loud, even when she whispers. I know Max heard her, but he ignores her and helps himself to a piece of strawberry cake and a slice of chocolate pie. He puts a huge bite of pie in his mouth and washes it down with some cake. Then he hands me a dessert plate.

I know Max is happy to be starting a new year with a lot of sweets and the girl of his dreams, but I can tell he's also happy to be starting it with me at home and not in the hospital.

It seems like all of my friends and family are glad I'm here. I watch while everyone helps themselves to cookies and cakes and pies. I still have to eat "soft" foods, which doesn't mean lots of dessert, but just knowing that the party didn't start without me is a sweet enough way for me to start the New Year.

Mom passes around apple tarts. Then she puts down her serving fork. "Mallory, you should be resting," she says.

When Mom says that, my friends start screeching again.

"We almost forgot," says Taylor. "We have another surprise." She takes my arm and leads me into the living room. My pillow and blanket from my bed are all nicely set up on the couch.

"You brought my bed in here!" I say.

Carine smiles. "We knew you would need to rest when you came home, and we wanted you to be nice and comfy while we watch the ball drop." My friends start tucking me in while Max turns on the TV.

We all watch the New Year's Eve festivities that took place in Times Square in New York City. After the ball drops and the New Year is officially welcomed, Max turns off the TV. "I'm out of here," says Max. He and Joey and Winnie go to his room, and all the grown-ups go into the dining room for coffee.

My friends and I are the only ones left in the living room.

"Thanks for all the surprises," I say.

They all smile and look at me like they were happy to do everything.

I feel so lucky to start off a new year with such great friends. But I also feel like my friends have been inside all morning. They must want to go outside. "If you want to go play in the snow, I totally understand," I tell them.

They all look at each other and then burst out laughing.

"We played in the snow all day yesterday," says Taylor.

"What we want is to spend the day with you," says Carine.

Mary Ann stands up and waves a DVD in my face. "Today is *spend-the-day-inside-with-Mallory-and-watch*-Fashion-Fran-*reruns* day," she says.

"But I thought you watched them yesterday," I say to Mary Ann.

Mary Ann puts the DVD in the TV and smiles at me. "Without you? No way!"

All my friends crowd around the couch as *Fashion Fran* comes on to the screen. We watch all afternoon.

While we're watching, Mary Ann lets me wear her teddy bear sweatshirt. It's so soft, and she knows how much I love it. Carine makes soup for me, and Taylor brings me a milk shake on a tray.

I smile at my friends. "When I was in the hospital, all I could think about was what I was missing. But you're all being so nice, it almost makes it seem like being in the hospital wasn't so bad." I stop talking for a minute. Then I say what has been on my mind ever since I came home. "Thanks so much for being such amazing friends."

My friends all give me big hugs.

I wish I hadn't had to have my appendix out, but being taken care of in such a nice way by my friends is a great way to start a new year. I lean back on my pillow and close my eyes. I think about the wish I made when I saw the wish pond this morning.

My reunion didn't go at all like I planned . . . but in lots of ways, the things I hadn't planned turned out to be even better than the things I had planned.

TEA FOR FOUR

"This is a lot more fun than the last tea party I had." I tell my friends about drinking clear fluid and eating Jell-O alone in the hospital.

"We're just glad you're OK," says Carine.

Taylor and Carine and Mary Ann and I all clink our teacups together. Actually, my cup is filled with tea and theirs are filled with hot chocolate. But I'm so happy to be home having a tea party in my room with my friends and not in the hospital drinking clear fluid all by myself that I don't care what my cup is filled with.

"I can't believe we're leaving today." Taylor pouts. "I feel like I just got here."

Actually, I *did* just get here. I still can't believe I missed half of the reunion, but the half I was at was super fun. I feel so lucky to have such good friends.

I put down my cup. "Thanks again for being so sweet when I came home from the hospital yesterday," I say to Taylor, Carine, and Mary Ann. "I loved all of my surprises. The sign and the soup and the milk shake and waiting to celebrate New Year's Eve were so nice. And I still can't believe you didn't mind staying inside with me all day instead of playing outside in the snow."

Carine and Taylor and Mary Ann all look at each other and start giggling.

All of a sudden, I feel like there's
something they know that I don't. Maybe
they gave me another surprise and I was
so tired from the operation, I don't even
remember it. "Did I forget something?" I
ask my friends.

"No," says Mary Ann. "We did. We have
another surprise for you."

"Another one!" I feel like I've had so
many surprises already.

"We think you're going to like this one a lot," says Taylor. She and Mary Ann and Carine stand up and open the curtains so I can see out my window.

When they do, I can't believe what I'm seeing. Four snow girls. They all have on name tags. *Carine. Taylor. Mary Ann. Mallory.* They're even wearing our real hats and scarves.

"I love them!" I gasp. "It must have taken you all day to make them. They're so big, and they look so much like us."

Carine puts her arm around me. "We wanted them to be just right. We spent a long time outside making them."

Taylor smiles. "That's why we didn't mind staying inside yesterday."

Now it's my turn to smile. When I was in the hospital, I thought everyone had forgotten all about me. But seeing the snow girls means my friends were thinking about me the whole time I was gone. "I love them, and I'm glad you spent a lot of time outside in the snow." I pretend pout. "Even if I wasn't there."

Mary Ann points to the Mallory snow girl. "But you were there," she says with a laugh.

Mary Ann, Taylor, and Carine all laugh. "Good friends always stick together," says Mary Ann.

"Even when one of them has to go to the hospital." Carine gives me a big hug.

"Oh no!" I shout.

Carine drops her arms. "Did I hug you too tight? Are you OK? I don't want to hurt you."

"No!" I tell Carine. "You didn't hurt me."
Now it's my turn to laugh. "It's just that I
forgot that I have something for you too!"

Carine, Taylor, and Mary Ann all look
confused and like they're waiting for me to
explain.

And I do. "I forgot that I have surprises
for you too." I pull a little bag out of my
top drawer, and open it up. I take out four
pink glass hearts on black cords. Now, I'm
really glad Mom made me stop at the gift
shop in the hospital and get something
for my friends. I start tying the necklaces
around my friends' necks. "We can all

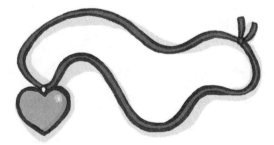

wear them until we see each other at camp next summer."

Taylor gives me a big hug. "They're like friendship necklaces."

Carine hugs me again, but not so tight this time. "I'm not going to take mine off until I see all of you at camp next summer."

Mary Ann ties a necklace around my neck. "Let's make a pinkie swear," she says.

We all wrap our pinkies together. *We pinkie swear not to take off our friendship necklaces until we're back at Camp Blue Lake next summer.*

While we're busy pinkie swearing, Grandma comes into my room. "It looks like you girls are having a wonderful time," she says.

"We are," I tell her. "We're just sad that it's about to end in a few minutes when Carine's dad gets here."

Grandma nods her head like she
understands how hard it is to say good-bye.

"I know how you feel. I'm leaving in
a few minutes too. But, as they say,
all good things must come to an end."
Grandma makes an *I'm-sad-to-go* face.
Then she holds up a basket of apple
cinnamon muffins. "But before this party

ends, I hope you'll
all find a little
room for some
muffins to go
with your hot
chocolate."

"Are they
Mallory
muffins?" asks
Taylor.

Grandma
winks at me.

"Mallory muffins are the only kind I ever make."

Taylor takes a muffin out of the basket and takes a bite. "They taste even better than they smell!"

"We're sure going to miss your grandma's baking," says Carine.

I can tell Grandma likes hearing that. She loves when people love her baked goods. Grandma puts the muffin basket down on my desk and then starts to leave.

"Grandma, wait." I get to my door before she does and block the way so she can't leave. "Do you want to stay and have tea with us?" I ask.

Grandma smiles. "Girls, you enjoy your tea party. I'm going to go finish packing. Anyway, it looks like you're having a good time having tea for four."

"Grandma, a very smart lady told me that tea can be for as many people as you want it to be for." I wink at Grandma, and she laughs.

Then she gives me a big hug. "Mallory, I think I've heard that one before," says Grandma.

RESOLUTIONS

Dad passes around a plate of grilled cheese sandwiches. "Who's ready for school to start tomorrow?" he asks.

Max takes a big bite out of his sandwich. "Dad, do you actually expect someone to raise their hand and say yes?"

Mom ladles tomato soup into bowls and passes them around the table. "Actually, I'm kind of ready to get back to school and see my students," says Mom.

Max rolls his eyes. "That sounds like

something a teacher would say."

I take a little bite out of my sandwich and feed a bite to Cheeseburger under the table. "Well, I'm not a teacher and I'm kind of ready to get back to school too."

Max groans like he can't imagine why I would say something like that. But I ignore him and talk to Mom and Dad.

"Even though parts of the holidays were fun, like having Grandma and my friends come visit, other parts, like getting my appendix out, weren't so much fun. I'm ready to leave the old year behind and start a new one."

Dad pushes his plate back and clears his throat. "Mallory, I'm glad you said what you did about starting a new year. With all of the excitement over the holidays, I just realized that the McDonald family never made their New Year's resolutions."

Max groans again like he really doesn't like where this conversation is going. "I have a resolution," says Max. "I resolve to put a sock in Mallory's mouth if she doesn't learn when to keep it shut."

"Max!" Mom and Dad both say his name at the same time.

You don't have to be the class brain to know that my parents don't like my brother's New Year's resolution. "I have a resolution," I say.

Mom and Dad look at me like they can't wait to hear what it is.

"I resolve to never get my appendix out again."

Dad smiles. "Since you only have one appendix and it's gone, I don't think that will be a problem."

I take another bite of my sandwich. "OK. Then I resolve to find some other way to

get people to bring me milk shakes and soup while I lie on the couch."

"I'll do the same thing," says Max.

Mom and Dad both laugh. Then Dad gets a serious look on his face. "I think all the McDonalds need to think of New Year's resolutions that are important to them."

All of a sudden, the McDonald dinner table is a very quiet place.

"I have a resolution," says Mom. She puts her fork down. "I resolve to spend more time having fun with my family."

Mom looks at me. I almost never see her cry, but it looks like she has tears in her eyes. "Being in the hospital with Mallory made me think how lucky we all are. We should enjoy and make the most of the good times."

Dad clears his throat. "I don't want to

be unoriginal, but I like Mom's resolution, and I'm going to make the same one."

My parents give Max a *you're-the-oldest-child-so-you're-next* look.

Max taps his fingers on the table like he's thinking. "Can I make the same resolution?"

Mom smiles at Max. "C'mon Max, get serious."

My brother almost never looks serious, but he does right now. I can tell he's trying hard to think of something. I can also tell he can't think of a thing. But I can. "Is it OK if I go first?" I ask my parents.

"Of course," says Dad.

Max looks relieved.

I push my plate back and clear my throat like Dad did. "My New Year's resolution is to learn to take the bad with the good."

Mom looks at me like that's not something she expected me to say. "Mallory, what do you mean?" she asks.

"Well, *taking the bad with the good* is an expression that Mrs. Daily taught us last year. She said it means that some days and things are better than others and that you have to enjoy the good things when you get them, but be prepared to handle the bad." I pause and look at my family. They're all quiet like they're waiting for me to finish my explanation, so I do.

"I don't think I really knew what she meant until now. I was so excited for all of my friends to come and visit, and I made so many fun plans. Then I thought everything was ruined when I had to go to the hospital to have my appendix out. But when I came home, all my friends surprised me with all the nice things they did for me. The reunion didn't go the way I had planned, but it was still great."

"Mallory, I think that is a wonderful resolution," says Mom. "Sometimes, things don't go as planned, and when that happens, oftentimes our only choice is just to accept what comes our way and make the best of it."

"And sometimes things don't go as planned, and it turns out to be a good thing," I add.

Dad rumples my hair. "Mallory, you're right," he says.

Max clears his throat like it's his turn to talk. "I don't want to be unoriginal. But I like Mallory's resolution." He looks at me. "If it's OK with you, I'm going to make the same one."

I smile. Max never likes what I do.
"Sure," I say with a big smile.

Max smiles like he's happy too. I'm not
sure if it's because he doesn't have to think
of his own resolution or because we're
getting along, but either way, it's a great
way to start a new year.

I look at Mom. "I think I know what you

meant in the hospital when you said that when life hands you lemons, you have to make lemonade."

Mom stands up and gasps. "Mallory, thank you for saying that. I almost forgot something important!" She walks over to the refrigerator. "Everyone, close your eyes."

I hear the refrigerator door open and shut.

"OK," says Mom. "Everyone can open their eyes."

When I do, Mom puts a giant lemon meringue pie on the table. Mom winks at me. "Mallory, I'm glad you listened to what I had to say. But sometimes, when life hands you lemons, you have to make lemon pie!"

Everyone laughs as Mom cuts thick slices of pie and passes them around the table.

"I think making lemon pie out of lemons is a great idea!" I say as I take a big bite.

Max eats the piece Mom cuts for him. When he's done, he clears his throat. "Is it OK if I make another resolution?" he asks Dad.

"Of course!" Dad nods like he loves that idea.

"I resolve to eat another piece of pie," says Max.

I put down my fork. "I don't want to be unoriginal. But is it OK if I make the same resolution as Max?"

We all laugh as we eat.

I don't think it has anything to do with the pie, but something tells me this is going to be a very sweet year.

A SPECIAL SCRAPBOOK

Mary Ann made a superspecial scrapbook for me of our winter reunion. Here are some of my favorite things in it.

A picture of me (with my appendix) and Carine, Mary Ann, and Taylor when they all arrived.

A picture of me (without my appendix) on the couch on New Year's Day.

A picture of Murphy, Cheeseburger, and Champ on New Year's Day.

And last, but definitely not least, a picture of me with my friends wearing our friendship necklaces.

Mary Ann says we look cute, cute, cute, cute. That's one cute for each girl.

Pictures aren't the only things Mary Ann put in my scrapbook. She put in some recipes too!

TAYLOR'S AMAZING CHOCOLATE MILK SHAKE

3 scoops chocolate ice cream
1 BIG squeeze of chocolate syrup
1/2 cup of milk
whipped cream

In blender, combine ice cream, syrup, and milk, and blend until smooth. Pour into tall glass, and top with whipped cream. Sip and say, *Mmmm!*

CARINE'S CHICKEN NOODLE SOUP

For an amazing bowl of soup, follow these 6 simple steps:

Step #1: Open a can of chicken noodle soup.

Step #2: Heat according to directions on the package.

Step #3: Pour soup into a bowl.

Step #4: Place bowl on a tray with a napkin and a spoon.

Step #5: Add crackers and your favorite beverage (apple juice works well).

Step #6: Eat up and enjoy!

Even though looking at these pictures and reading these recipes makes me a little sad that our winter reunion is over, I love having it and I think it was really nice of Mary Ann to make the scrapbook for me.

And the good news is . . . it will really come in handy. I won't see Carine and Taylor until camp starts next summer, which is in exactly five months, three weeks, two days, and I'm not sure how many hours and minutes.

But until then, at least I have a scrapbook to look at that's filled with lots of happy memories.

 **MALLORY'S INBOX**

Now that the reunion is over and Grandma and my friends are gone, there isn't as much excitement in my house. At least I have a full inbox!

Subject: I.M.U! (I miss you!)
From: carineluvsgreen
To: malgal

Mallory,
Thanks so much for planning such a great winter reunion. It was so much fun (even though we didn't get to see you as much as we wanted to). I wish your appendix had picked a different time (or better yet, no time) to need to come out. I hope you're feeling much better!
Love, Carine

Subject: Next summer!
From: taylortalks
To: malgal, chatterbox, carineluvsgreen

Mallory, Mary Ann, and Carine,

I'm so, so, so sad our winter reunion is over. But guess what? It got me so, so, so excited for next summer at Camp Blue Lake. I can't believe we have to wait almost 6 whole months to be together again. I will be counting the days, weeks, and minutes.
I miss you all already!

Loads of luv, Taylor

P.S. Mallory, tell Cheeseburger that I miss her too!

Subject: Going back to school
From: chatterbox, boardboy
To: malgal

Mallory,

We can't believe winter break is over, the snow has melted, and tomorrow we go back to school. There's only one thing we have to say about that . . . Boo hoo! Boo hoo! Boo hoo! Actually, that was three things, but we felt like saying it.

See you in the morning on the way to school!

Mary Ann and Joey

P.S. Hey Mallory, it's Joey. I bet you can tell that Mary Ann wrote most of this email!

Subject: I'm proud of you!
From: maxandmallory'sdad
To: malgal

Mallory,

I know it's a little unusual for me to send you an email, but I thought you might like getting one from your dad.

I wanted to tell you again how proud I am of you for making the best of a bad situation. I know it was no fun having your appendix out, especially when you were supposed to be having fun with your friends. But you said it best, you turned a lemon into lemonade.

That's my girl!

I love you,
Dad

AN EMAIL FROM MALLORY

Subject: Starting a New Year!
From: malgal
To: Anyone reading this letter (and that includes you!)

I just wanted to say *Happy New Year!*
You never know what's going to happen when you start something new, especially something big, like a year. But I hope everything that happens to you this year is great. And if it's not, I hope you find an OK way of dealing with it.

If you want to do something special to kick off your year, you can try doing what I did and make a resolution to make things as great as you can make them no matter what happens. And if you don't want to do that, well, I'm sure you can think up something on your own. There are lots of good ways to start a new year.

I can't believe I'm leaving behind an old year (and in my case, an appendix too), and starting a new one. When I'm done with this email, I'm going straight to the wish pond on my street and making a wish that there will be lots of fun things to look forward to this year and hopefully some surprises (the good kind) too!

I'm going to make the same wish for you.

Happy New Year and big, huge hugs and kisses!
Mallory

Carolrhoda Books
A division of Lerner Publishing Group, Inc.
241 First Avenue North
Minneapolis, MN 55401 U.S.A.

Website address: www.lernerbooks.com

Library of Congress Cataloging-in-Publication Data

Friedman, Laurie B., 1964–
      Happy New Year, Mallory! / by Laurie Friedman ; illustrations by Jennifer Kalis.
          p.   cm.
      Summary: When a bad stomachache sends Mallory to the hospital during a winter reunion with neighbor Mary Ann and their summer camp bunkmates, she is sad that her friends seem to be having great fun without her.
      ISBN: 978-0-8225-8883-2 (trade hardcover : alk. paper)
      [1. Reunions—Fiction. 2. Friendship—Fiction. 3. Sick—Fiction. 4. Family life—Fiction. 5. New Year—Fiction.] I. Kalis, Jennifer, ill. II. Title.
   PZ7.F89773Has 2009
   [Fic]—dc22   2008041164

Manufactured in the United States of America
2 — BP — 12/1/09